THE VERY NOISY BEAR

NICK BLAND

Scholastic Canada Ltd.

Toronto New York London Auckland Sydney
Mexico City New Delhi Hong Kong Buenos Aires

For Nanna

Scholastic Canada Ltd.
604 King Street West, Toronto, Ontario M5V 1E1, Canada

Scholastic Inc.
557 Broadway, New York, NY 10012, USA

Scholastic Australia Pty Limited
PO Box 579, Gosford, NSW 2250, Australia

Scholastic New Zealand Limited
Private Bag 94407, Botany, Manukau 2163, New Zealand

Scholastic Children's Books
Euston House, 24 Eversholt Street, London NW1 1DB, UK

www.scholastic.ca

Nick used acrylic paint on paper to create these illustrations.

Library and Archives Canada Cataloguing in Publication
Bland, Nick, 1973-, author
The very noisy bear / Nick Bland.

ISBN 978-1-4431-4662-3 (bound).--ISBN 978-1-4431-4663-0 (pbk.)
I. Title.
PZ10.3.B527 Ven 2015   j823'.92   C2015-901730-0

6 5 4 3 2 1   Printed in Malaysia 108   15 16 17 18 19

In the Jingle Jangle Jungle,
there was music in the air . . .

And it landed in the ears
of a very sleepy Bear.

"Excuse me!" said the bear
to the music-making sheep.
"Your band is very noisy
and it's time for me to sleep."

"Now that you're awake,"
said Sheep, "perhaps
you'd like to stay?

Have you ever tried the jungle drums?
They're really fun to play."

Lion was on the jungle drums and Bear began to smile.
"I suppose if I could play the drums, I'd stay a little while."

He sat upon the tiny stool.

BOOM
BANG
BASH!

BOOM went the noisy Bear.

BOOM
BANG—

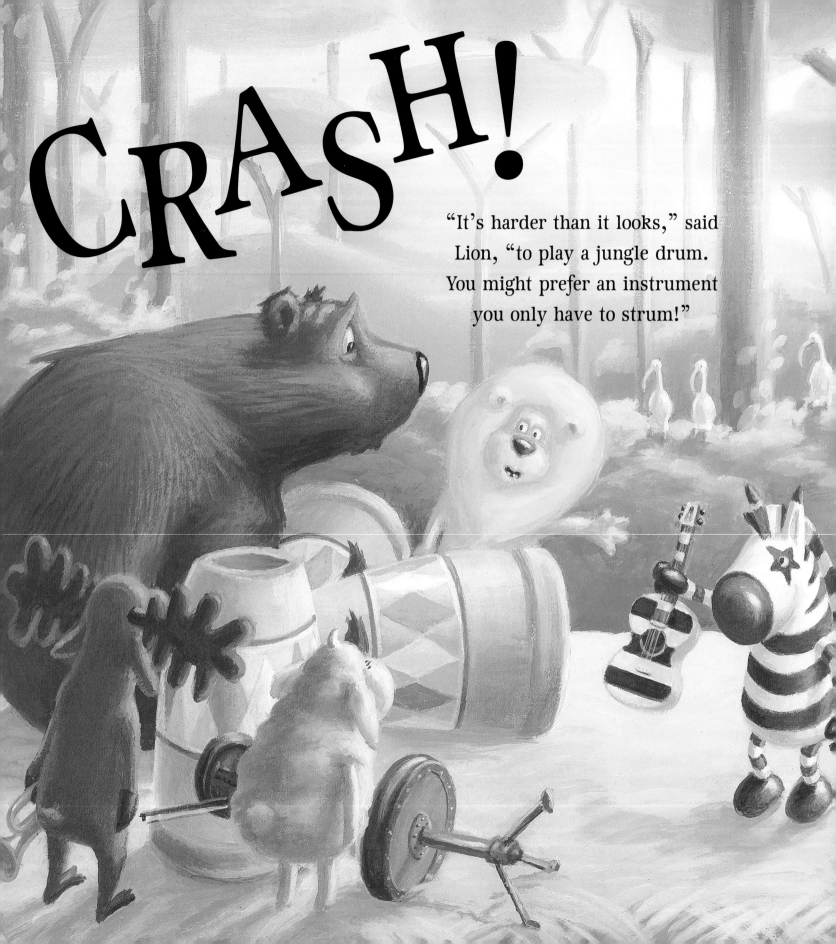

CRASH!

"It's harder than it looks," said Lion, "to play a jungle drum. You might prefer an instrument you only have to strum!"

Zebra had a striped guitar.
She handed it to Bear.

"You hold it over here," she said,
"and strum it over there."

Bear started strumming gently,
but it wasn't very loud.

Then he strummed a little harder,
so the sound could reach the crowd.

But his claws were
long and curly
and they tangled
in the strings.

"Never mind," said Zebra.
"Guitars are tricky things."

Moose held up his trumpet.
"Would you like to have a go?

All you have to do," he said,
"is take a breath and blow!"

Bear took in a **giant** breath . . .

and *blew* with all his might.
The trumpet made a SCREECHING noise
and all the birds took flight!
The elephants stampeded and all the monkeys left.

SCREECH

Everyone took cover . . .
until Bear was out of breath.

"Your lungs are awfully strong," said Sheep. "You must be very proud.
But there *is* another instrument that isn't quite as loud.

Have you ever tried a microphone? It's just a simple thing.
You only have to hold it up, clear your throat and sing!"

She handed Bear the microphone and counted up to four.
The band began to play a tune and Bear began to . . .

"ROAR!"

"Roar!" went the noisy Bear,
   "Roar! Roar! Roar!"

"More!" cheered the audience,
   "More! More! More!"

The elephants were dancing
and the monkeys sang along.
He roared in perfect harmony
through every single song.

Then when the show was over
and the moon had settled in,
when everyone was fast asleep . . .

. . . he tried the violin!